MW00889245

5-MINUTE

MODERN-DAY
CHRISTIAN
BEDTIME STORIES
FOR RAISING DISCIPLES

VOLUME 1

SAVANNAH BLOOM

NOTE TO PARENTS

The stories you are about to read may be different than you expect. They are short stories set in today's society but with whimsical elements based on new technology or wild imaginations. I've set out to show examples of character-building in progress. Sometimes characters make a poor choice, and sometimes they learn the hard way or are scared or regretful. **In every story, good character is rewarded or promoted, and character flaws are revealed and dealt with.**

Also, while I've tried to balance realism, fantasy, and age-appropriateness, I wanted to give you a heads up that **there are a few elements that may be intense for 4-5 year-olds (i.e. an eagle attack, scooter injuries, walking toward doom, past jail-time, etc.)** I'd advise a quick scan of the stories before you read-aloud.

Finally, with this first Christ-centered volume, I'm hoping to avoid the more-controversial topics while sticking to God's character and the central truths that bring children closer to Him. If you'd like to know, I have background in Evangelical-Free, Baptist, and Pentecostal churches, and I've read NIV, KJV, ESV, and NLT Bibles.

I trust that YOU will take these stories and use/adapt them to your child's current understanding. I am praying that this book will be another tool in your toolbelt as you work to share Jesus' truth and love with your child during precious night times.

In parental solidarity,

Savannah Bloom

TABLE OF CONTENTS

THE GOOD SAMIR IS HERE!

LOVE YOUR NEIGHBOR

LUKE 10:30-37

In tonight's story, Lark discovers that the most helpful and loving people aren't always the ones you expect.

Not long ago, there was a girl named Lark who loved her hover-scooter. Day after day she would ride it around her neighborhood. She would wave at any neighbors she saw, especially Chris, the Boy Scout.

"Hey, Chris!"

"Hey!" he replied, with his usual bright smile. His Boy Scout uniform looked especially sharp today. He was her favorite neighbor, mostly because he sold her family caramel popcorn during the holidays and was always sporting that cheery smile.

Her other neighbors were friendly, too, but some were too busy to wave back.

"Hey, Pamela!"

Pamela smiled and nodded.

Pamela lived across from Lark and was always driving from one place to another. She was very busy leading committees and projects and businesses. Maybe it was because she was so busy and in a hurry that she never waved.

Then there was Samir who lived in the biggest, three-story mansion at the end of the road. His dad wore a hat called a turban, and he believed there were lots of gods instead of just one – at least that's what Lark's mother told her he believed. Lark had never really spoken to Samir. Lark was a little nervous around him, but he waved again as she sped past hovering a few inches from the ground.

She ramped off a few curbs, popped a few wheelies, and spun a few 360's, but she soon tired of the same old stunts. She'd seen videos of other kids pulling off some amazing flips, and she longed to try them herself.

If only she had a big enough ramp, or a...

...a skate park! She lit up in excitement. That's what she needed! A skate park with ramps and half-pipes and rails! And it just happened that there was a skate-park in the city, just down the highway a few miles.

She called her mom, but she didn't answer.

Lark would call her back later. But for now, she had to get started. It looked like there were storm clouds on the horizon. If she wanted to get some cool stunts in, she'd better hurry.

Zipping off at top speed, Lark smiled with excitement. The humid air rushed against her face, bringing thoughts to her mind of soaring through the air, twisting, falling toward the cement, then whooshing down the ramp at incredible speed only to do it on the other side. She closed her eyes for a moment, imagining it…

Her hoverboard dipped hard, into a pothole. Before she could react, she lost her grip and fell over the handlebars, skidding onto the street, banging her helmeted head before collapsing into a grassy ditch.

The clouds spun above her like twirling cotton candy. Then everything went dark.

She woke up with a throbbing headache. Groaning from the pain, she tried to right herself, but her legs hurt too much to stand. She collapsed from the effort and felt the crunch of something electronic in her back pocket.

"Oh no," she muttered, pulling out her broken phone.

The screen was shattered. It couldn't dial or hear her voice. Her mom wouldn't be able to help.

Maybe I can crawl to my scooter, she thought, spotting it on the side of the road. She crawled through the grass, grimacing in pain. But when she got closer, it became clear she wasn't going anywhere on the scooter. Its front was bent and twisted, sad and useless.

Lark began to cry, her tears falling down her cheeks. What could she do now? What could she do now, but cry and pray? She prayed for help for a long while and had nearly given up when headlights appeared.

Her heart leapt in relief.

"Help!" she cried.

The car rolled to a stop. It was Pamela. "Oh, dear! I would help, but I have a car full of food for the food pantry and a volunteer team waiting for me. A lot of people need my help! I'll call your mom the first chance I get!"

With that, Pamela sped off.

Lark was astounded. How could Pamela leave her like this?

At least Pamela would call her mom. But how long would she have to wait? Storm clouds were coming closer, too. It was already growing colder.

She shivered in pain and fear and cold.

Just then, a biker rolled up. It was Chris!

His bright smile vanished when he saw her condition. But then he looked at the rain clouds behind him. "I'm sorry, but I've got to get going. I'm giving a presentation on first aid, and if I'm late, I won't get my merit badge. Here's a box of cookies!"

Chris threw her a box of cookies before pedaling away.

"Wait! Help!" she pleaded.

But Chris kept pedaling.

Lark huffed. Maybe he wasn't as nice as she thought.

Thunder rumbled. Raindrops thumped her hair and prickled her wounds. Another shiver shuddered through her bones as she peered down the darkening highway.

Just when she had nearly given up hope, through the rain, she spotted another pair of headlights.

The car nearly passed by but skidded to a stop. The driver's fancy door swung upward, and there was Samir. He leapt out, immediately rushing to her aid. "Let's get you out of the rain."

Samir helped her to her feet and pulled her inside the fancy, self-driving car. It had to be expensive, but Samir didn't seem to care that she was getting it muddy and bloody. He even tore his expensive clothes to use as bandages for her wounds.

"There. That will do until we get you to the hospital. Car, call Mrs. Malloway."

"Thank you," Lark whispered, laying her head back in relief.

"You're welcome."

"I'm sorry about the mud, the rain, the blood, your clothes…"

"Never mind that," Samir said. "I'm just being a good neighbor."

THE END

FUN QUESTION

If you could choose five new neighbors to live in five places all around your place, who would you choose? Why?

OPTIONAL LESSON READING:

Did you know Jesus tells a story like this one, where an injured person is helped by someone unexpected and different? Jesus wants us to love people like Samir loved Lark. He wants us to see people as more important than all the other things going on in our lives. Let's be good neighbors like Samir, ready to help those around us!

SERIOUS DISCUSSION

Why didn't Pamela stop to help? Why didn't Chris stop to help? Do you ever make excuses for not helping others? What's an excuse that you make a lot, that you can start making less? (I'm too tired, don't want to, etc.)

Tomorrow's story has a character who counts his brother's sins!

SEVENTY-SEVEN SINS

UNLIMITED FORGIVENESS

MATTHEW 18:21

In tonight's story, Liam learns that putting limits on forgiveness can hurt his friendship with his brother.

Not long ago, Liam was building the highest, fastest toy car ramp he'd ever built. It started from his ceiling fan, zoomed to his dresser, looped and reversed around his desk and barreled into his trash can. The tracks were hung by scotch tape for now, until he could...

"Hey, Liam!" his brother, Noah, announced, opening the door like he was a superhero busting through a wall.

"Stop!" Liam warned, holding out his hand. "Don't touch the...!"

Noah touched the track. "Cool track!"

And just like that, the tape began to rip.

"No, no, no!" Liam tried to stop it. But Noah could only watch as the tracks ripped free and collapsed into a sticky mess.

"Sorry," Noah muttered.

"UGH!" Liam felt his anger boiling.

His little brother knew that look by now. He took off running, screaming for their mother. "Mommy!"

Their mother came to little Noah's rescue and hugged him tight.

"I said I was sorry!" Noah moaned from under his mother's protection.

Liam huffed. "You always say sorry, but you keep messing up my stuff!"

"I'm sorry!" Noah said again, starting to cry.

Their mother whispered, "Liam. If he apologizes, what should you do?"

Liam crossed his arms. "Forgive him. But I do that every time. How many times am I supposed to forgive him?"

His mother smiled. "Did you know that Peter asked Jesus that same question?" She found the nearest Bible and read the passage. *Then Peter came to Jesus and asked, "Lord, how many times shall I forgive my brother or sister who sins against me?"*

Jesus answered, "I tell you, not seven times, but seventy-seven times."

Liam's jaw dropped. "Seventy-seven times!" He couldn't believe it. That would take forever! He'd be forgiving his brother for months!

But then he had an idea. It was clever, and a little mischievous.

He smiled at his brother – a twisted smile. Then, when his mother had left, he took the black-light marker out. He knew this special marker's marks only showed up when the special black-light bulb was on.

He marked the wall, leaving what looked like an eerie green claw mark. "Seventy-six more sorries to go," he muttered to himself before clicking off the lamp.

The next day his brother bumped into him while he was carrying his cereal bowl. Milk splattered the floor.

"Sorry," Liam said.

"Oh, I forgive you," Noah said before rushing to his room, knowing that meant one more mark.

Three more times that very day, Liam said he was sorry. Once for entering the bathroom without knocking; once for hitting his trophies with his baseball; and once for kneeing him in the nose during a wrestling match.

After seeing all the day's green marks on the wall, Liam began liking Noah's apologies. He even tried to walk closer to him to earn a shoulder bump apology. Or he built his tracks near the door so a mere opening of the door would knock them over. Liam knew that each apology took him one closer to never having to forgive him again.

"Sorry," Noah said after a shoulder bump.

"I forgive you!" Liam chirped before running to his room.

But this time, he forgot to close the door. When he made his mark, he heard someone at the door, spying on him.

"Hey!" Liam yelled at his snooping brother, trying to hide the marks.

"Sorry! I didn't know…but what are those?"

Noah snickered, hearing another apology. He turned and made another mark, next to the other seventy marks.

"Are those…my sorries?" Noah asked, timidly walking closer.

"Yes – the ones I forgive," Liam replied in the glow of the lamp. "Seventy-one now. You have six forgivable sorries left."

Noah's face was crinkled in fear. "What happens when I run out?"

Liam leaned in. "We'll find out soon enough."

Noah ran from the room and acted strange the rest of the week. He avoided Liam like he was some sort of monster. When he walked past, he gave Liam a wide space, afraid of an accidental bump. He refused to wrestle anymore; and he never entered Liam's room.

At first, Liam liked the extra space. But it didn't take long to get lonely. As much as his brother annoyed him, Liam still loved the guy and liked playing with him.

"You still have six sorries left," Liam mentioned at breakfast.

Little Noah shrugged. "For like sixteen years. I'll need one for when I take your girlfriend."

Liam spit out a mouthful of cereal. "What?!"

Noah laughed and ran from the table, Liam rampaging behind him. "Oh, you'll be sorry, all right!"

But before Liam could grab his brother's shirt collar, their mother had corralled them both, shepherding them into her room. She sat them on her bed in silence until both had calmed down. "I want to show you both something."

She flicked off the light. And all about the dark room shown green marks, etching the walls from top to bottom like twigs building a giant dam on all sides.

"Whoa," they both exclaimed. "What are those for?" Noah asked.

"They are my sorries," she said. "To God."

"Huh?"

"I've had to ask Him for forgiveness more times than I can count. Many more times than 77. More than seventy times seven."

"And He keeps forgiving?" Liam asked.

"If He had a limit, I would be afraid to come near to Him, just like your brother has been afraid to mess up around you. But the grace of God has no limits. We can always come to him, say sorry, and because of what Jesus did for us, He'll…"

She flicked on the lights. The marks disappeared.

Liam thought on God's forgiveness and how many marks God could have made for him. "You know what, Noah? I'm sorry I kept track of your sorries."

Noah nodded, "You said *sorry*." Then he licked his finger and wiped a slimy mark on Liam's cheek. "That's one!" He ran away.

THE END

FUN QUESTION

If you had your parents' permission, what would you paint or draw on your bedroom walls?

OPTIONAL LESSON READING:

Did you know that Jesus told Peter not to count others' sins, but to forgive them as many times as He as forgiven us? And He has forgiven us many, many times – just like the marks on Liam's mother's walls show. Aren't you so glad that Jesus' forgiveness doesn't have a limit? Now we should make sure that we forgive others' the same way – without limits!

SERIOUS DISCUSSION

How does it make you feel that Jesus is waiting to forgive you – even if you sin over and over and over? Talk to Him now – and know He has no limits on your sorries!

Tomorrow's story has the most disgusting water park in the world!

THE SEEDY WATER PARK

SHARE THE GOOD NEWS

MATTHEW 13:1-9,18-23

*In tonight's story, Reena learns to share good news with everyone,
because someone will be happy to hear it.*

Not long ago, Reena was having a blast in the most disgusting water park in the world. Of course, she didn't know it was the most disgusting water park in the world. She, along with everyone else, thought all water parks were disgusting, painful, and generally uncomfortable.

The water was yellow, brown, a little black, and sometimes blue. Everything stunk, like wet gym socks filled with rotten beans. The glass roof was uneven, so sometimes sun would beam directly in your eyes or burn your skin if you stayed in one place for too long. The concession stand only sold stale pretzels, and every slide creaked like teeth on a fork – until the slide ran out of water. Then, the rider was stuck until the lifeguards could slosh an emergency bucket of grease down the slide to help the rider the rest of the way down.

Yet, people still came and still had fun. For many people, like Reena, it was as good as she thought a water park could get.

So she went down the creaking slides, she hopped across floating, slimy lily pads, and she climbed the play structure with the giant water bucket that tipped over with a waterfall of sudsy brown liquid.

She did her best never to swallow any of the stuff the water park called water. And she wore sunglasses under her goggles and extra sunscreen lotion to protect her from those shifty sun's rays. It was all working out to an okay day!

Then, on her way to get stale pretzels, she tried to clean her dirty goggles with her greasy towel which only made them worse. For a moment, she couldn't see.

"OOF!" She ran into someone and crumpled to the ground. Frazzled, she took off the greasy goggles and saw a happy boy in a clean, wet swimsuit. Blue and clear water dripped from his soaking hair.

"Oh, sorry!" he said, excitedly. "I didn't see you. I was just so excited. I have to tell everyone!"

"Huh?" Reena asked, trying to push herself up. As she did so, her hand fell on a paper with colorful words and slides on it. She held it up, perplexed. At the top, it read, "KINGDOM WATER PARK. It's better than you can imagine!"

And the pictures looked unreal. The slides had gushing blue water. The pools were clear. The roof was even. There were smiling kids with baskets of burgers, fries, cheese balls, and ice cream treats.

"It's true," the boy said, offering her a helping hand. He helped her up. "I was just there. It's amazing. Glorious. Heavenly compared to…this." He swept his hand toward the place. Then he made a face. "And it doesn't stink."

Reena gasped. Could it be true? How had she not heard of this place? "Is this a joke or something?"

"No! And it's not a secret. I've got to tell everyone. It's open to anyone who is willing to give this place up."

Reena laughed. "Well, that should be everyone!" Reena couldn't imagine anyone saying no to such an unbelievably amazing waterpark.

"Can you help me spread the word?" the boy asked. "Tell everyone the good news! There's a shuttle bus that'll take anyone who wants to go, but it leaves in ten minutes!"

Reena jumped to action, following the boy, both shouting at the top of their lungs. "Come, see the most amazing water park EVER! It doesn't stink!"

"Huh?" a little girl asked as the giant water bucket gushed its dirty load.

"What are they saying?" an older lady asked over the sound of creaking slides.

"THERE'S A BETTER WATER PARK!" Reena shouted.

The woman shrugged. "Stop shouting. If you don't like this place, just leave."

"But…" Reena began.

The boy pulled her away. "Some might not understand, but we don't have time. We have to try others." Then he turned toward a group of tables where families gathered to dry off and eat stale pretzels.

"COME! SEE! A clean water park for all!"

"Really?" a father asked. A whole family seemed interested. The boy handed them more of the papers. Their eyes were ablaze with wonder. "We can go here? They'll let us in? Even if we're so…dirty?" The father looked ashamed of their greasy, gross appearance.

"Sure! Come!" said the boy. "There are showers to make you clean."

But suddenly, a group of lifeguards came swooping in, grabbing the papers. "You can't pass these out here! It's not allowed! Besides, there's no such thing as clean water parks."

The lifeguards left as quickly as they came. And the family quickly dispersed, suddenly more afraid of the lifeguards than excited for the Kingdom.

But the boy did not give up. "COME! SEE!" he bellowed to a large group. "A water park with slides that work!"

Another group of families listened and began walking toward the shuttle bus in excitement. But worries began to pop up.

"What if this is a scam, and they try to make us pay for towels and every little thing?" one worried as he wandered away.

"Or what if it's too crowded? Let's just stay here. At least we know this is kind of fun." Another family chose to stay.

But not all of them were taken away by worries. Some believed the boy and what he had seen. They followed him even as lifeguards and others began to mock them, throw things at them, and push them out the door.

But Reena stood firm with the boy and the others all the way to the shuttle bus and then to Kingdom Water Park.

And indeed, it was better than they could have imagined.

THE END

FUN QUESTION

Can you think of any rides or slides at a yucky water park that could be fun? (ex – mustard hot tub, refried bean pit, etc.)

OPTIONAL LESSON READING:

Did you know that Jesus told a story where a farmer is planting seeds, but birds take some away – while other seeds don't grow in rocky or shallow soil? The story is meant to teach us that telling others about Jesus can be hard and frustrating, but that we shouldn't give up. Let's tell others how great Jesus is – just like that boy told others how great Kingdom Water park is!

SERIOUS DISCUSSION

Have you told anyone about God or Jesus? For some people, it can be a little scary to share. For others, it is exciting to share the good news that Jesus came to rescue us from sin – and He's preparing a place for us with Him in heaven (that's better than a water park). Who could you tell next?

Tomorrow's story has twins who love to compete in everything they do!

No, You're The Best!

Showing Honor

Romans 12:10

In tonight's story, Eli and Alex learn that competing to honor and serve someone best can be fun and rewarding.

Not long ago, twins, Eli and Alex, were making pancakes. It was easy enough. Pour the batter on the hot griddle, flip the pancake when the bubbles stop popping, then voila! Soon, they had a large stack that wobbled on the plate.

Eli started to grab the plate to carry it to the table, but Alex stopped him. "Wait," he said with excitement. "I bet I can get fling them onto the plates from here."

Eli glanced at the table where their family's plates were. A smirk worked its way to his mouth. "I bet I can fling more onto Dad's plate than you can on Mom's."

That was all it took for pancakes to go flying. Eli hit the syrup over. Alex's first pancake plopped into orange juice. Then Eli got one on his plate. Alex whipped his pancake, trying to strike Eli's off. But the zipping, flimsy frisbee-of-a-cake flew into the living room, slapping the TV.

Their dad rose from the couch.

"Uh-oh," they both muttered.

Later, after a stern talking-to, the boys raced to the bus, pushing and shoving through the others waiting in line.

"I won!"

"No, I won!"

A bus driver's husky voice broke in. "You both won seats up front and a note to your teacher."

But even that didn't stop the twins' love for competition. They raced through school assignments, even if that meant horrible handwriting. They made lunch into a game, with points for the most peas eaten and extra points for the most chicken nuggets in their mouth at the same time.

Alex won that game with twenty-three nuggets. He was sad that the nuggets ended up in chunks on the floor after he laughed like a garbage disposal, but the victory was worth it.

The twins were competitive in everything they did. It made life more fun and challenging. It was only natural that they loved sports as well.

Soccer practice was right after school, and both boys gave extra effort, hoping Coach would see their skills and put them on the starting team for the team's first game. Alex juggled the ball six times before punting it over the bleachers. Eli juggled it seven times before punting it over the bleachers – and onto Coach's car.

The ball landed with a metallic *THUNK* that left a ball-sized dent right in the middle.

"Uh oh."

Coach took them aside, twitching his eyebrows in restrained anger. "You two are very gifted."

"Aw, shucks," Eli said.

"But you're very misguided."

"What's that mean?"

"It means you're using your gifts in the wrong way. Instead of using your abilities to *do good*, you're using them to prove how good *you are*."

"Huh?"

Coach sighed. "Look. Romans 12:10 asks us to outdo one another in showing honor. That's the competition I want you two to focus on tonight and tomorrow. Outdo one another in showing each other honor – that's showing respect; serving one another; putting each other's needs before your own."

"So, like, who can be the better servant?"

Coach nodded. "Jesus came to serve. Who can be most like Jesus to his brother? Whoever wins can start this weekend's game."

Alex looked at Eli. Eli looked at Alex. Their looks turned to fierce glares. It was on.

The next morning was a lot different. Alex rolled out of bed quietly, but Eli heard him and jumped from the top bunk. They grabbed and fought each other all the way to the kitchen until Eli got the first piece of bread in the toaster.

"Ha! I will make you the best breakfast!"

"No way!" Alex retorted. "I will make you bacon. Beat that!"

The two laughed as they raced around the kitchen, outdoing one another for breakfast.

Alex put toothpaste on Eli's toothbrush. Eli put shampoo on Alex's hair. Alex pre-wadded a bunch of toilet paper and set it by the toilet for Eli. Eli laid out Alex's school clothes. Alex packed Eli a snack, with a note that said, "Best brother ever!"

They raced to the bus door, only to stop at the entrance, fighting over who went first. "After you!" "No, after you!"

The bus driver's jaw dropped at the display.

The competition heated up at school. Alex wiped down Eli's desk. Eli cleaned Alex's stinky locker. Alex offered to help with Eli's homework. Eli offered to bring Alex's lunch to his table for him.

And lunch was much calmer that day. In fact, the whole day went smoother. They didn't get in trouble one bit.

So, when they came before Coach, each one was confident they had won the competition.

"Boys. Did you learn anything from this?"

Alex shrugged. "It was cool. It can be kind of fun to serve someone."

Eli agreed. "Yeah. It was cool to see that Alex is such a cool guy."

"No, you're cooler."

"You're cooler!"

Coach huffed. "That's enough. Want to know who won?"

Alex waved it off. "That's okay. Eli can have the spot. He deserves it."

"No, you deserve it!"

"No, you do!"

Coach sighed. "You both win, if one of you is willing to play defender. Damon is sick."

Both boys chimed at the same time. "I'm willing!"

Coach smiled. "That's what I like to hear. You both love to compete, and that's okay – especially on the soccer field. But I hope you learned showing honor and respect is more important than any competition."

"I learned that Coach," Eli said. "But I bet Alex learned it better."

"No," Alex huffed. "You learned it better!"

"You did!"

"You did!"

Coach sighed and walked away with a smile.

THE END

FUN QUESTION

What are some fun competitions you can do around the house? (ex - who can get to sleep the fastest?)

OPTIONAL LESSON READING:

Did you know, in the book of Romans, Paul challenges Christians to outdo one another in showing honor? He wants brothers and sisters to challenge one another to see who can be the best servant. If Christians work together as teammates to become better and better at loving, serving, and honoring others – everyone will win!

SERIOUS DISCUSSION

Who is your favorite person to compete with? Who would win the competition to serve one another the best? Why?

Tomorrow's story has a boy who protects his safe with drones, poison gas, and sharks!

SAFE IN SAFE?

RICHES FADE

LUKE 12:15-21

In tonight's story, Jackson finds out that riches can be taken away at any time – so it's best to use them for good while you can.

Not long ago, Jackson's family moved to a farm. While digging in his backyard, Jackson's shovel hit something with a CLANG! His younger brother, Silas, stopped digging and ran over. "Whatcha hit? Dino bone? Treasure chest? Gas line?"

Jackson kept digging. "Don't know yet. Help me out!"

Together, the two boys dug around the object until it was revealed to be a giant rock. But it was no ordinary rock. It was glittering with golden ripples.

"WHOA! GOLD!" Jackson exclaimed.

"What do we do?" Silas asked.

"This whole yard could be filled with more gold!" Jackson whispered, as if someone could overhear. "We have to find it all."

Silas moaned. "But my hands hurt already. It'll take forever to dig the whole yard."

Jackson rolled his eyes. "Not if we're *rich*, Silas. We use this puny amount of gold to buy an excavator."

Sure enough, the next day, their new excavator was digging up the entire yard finding giant gold nuggets in every scoop.

"We're rich! Set for life! We can retire this very minute!" declared Jackson.

Silas arched a brow. "Retire? You mean, stop working? I've hardly started. I'm taking my gold and going to do great things with it. I'll help the world. Build hospitals, cure cancer, invent space weapons that can deflect earth-destroying asteroids – that kind of stuff."

"Okay, okay, you do that," Jackson said, heaving a gold nugget toward his house. "I'm going to keep my gold safe – IN a safe – the SAFEST safe in the world. So – when you run out of gold, you can come crawling back to me."

Jackson ordered the most secure safe known to man and a small army of workers brought it with a crane. They placed it in a shed and attached steel plates to the roof. They buried electrified fencing under the ground on all sides. Laser turrets were installed on the roof. And a watery moat was dug around the perimeter, with sharks patrolling to keep any intruders out.

The shed safe was more secure than any other place in the city – even more than the bank's vaults. And Jackson was the only one who could access it. To enter, he had to speak a password, put his eye and palm to the scanner, and spit into a cup. The computer analyzed his voice, eye, palm, and spit to make sure that it was really him. If it was, the vault door opened, allowing him to see his vast collection of gold.

He often did so, just to gaze at the glittering rocks. A few he had to sell to pay for all the security, and a few more he used to buy a video game system and movie theater for his home. Finally, he hired a McDonalds chef and had him make him food every day. After that, though, he didn't touch his gold.

Still, he wasn't satisfied. He was scared someone would take it from him and ruin everything. He wanted even more security. More!

So, he had the safe buried deep underground. Only an elevator could reach it. And the elevator was filled with poisonous gas. Someone would need a special suit to go inside. And the special suit was locked inside another vault with booby traps ready to go off if someone guessed the wrong answers to the trivia questions.

"WHAT IS JACKSON'S MIDDLE NAME?" it would ask.

Michael, you say? WRONG ANSWER! Arrow in the knee!

"WHAT IS JACKSON'S FAVORITE FOOD?"

Broccoli, you say? Trap door into lava!

"WHAT IS JACKSON'S FAVORITE COLOR?"

Gold, you say? Correct answer.

Jackson had drones patrol the outside and the inside. He bought armed robots to fire on anyone who lingered in the yard too long. And he made sure the safe would survive any earthquake, nuclear blast, flood, volcanic eruption, zombie apocalypse, or climate change that could happen.

After all that, he felt the safe was safe. His gold was safe.

His comfort, his pleasure, his good life and future was safe.

He thought to himself, *I have enough gold to last the rest of my life. I will eat McDonalds, play video games, watch movies, and be happy. And my gold will stay safe for me if I ever need it.*

He went to sleep without a worry for the first time.

And it was that night that he was taken.

He was taken. Not his gold.

Jackson was wrapped in a blanket, thrown in a chest, and hauled away.

For a long moment he thought he was dead. He cried out in despair. He had put all his hope in his gold. He thought having gold and keeping gold was all that mattered, but really, now that he had lost it all, maybe even his life – he wished he had done it differently.

He should have followed Silas' example. He should have used the gold to do great things for God, to help people - so that God could be proud of him. But now, if he died, what would God say? "You dug up Gold and then buried it again? What a fool!"

No, God wouldn't say that, but maybe Jackson deserved that. He'd been foolish. If he were given a second chance – if he could somehow get out of this chest alive, he would...

Light struck Jackson's eyes as the chest opened. Silas was smiling at him. "Silas?"

"Hey! Tricked ya! It's just me. I thought I'd rescue you from that boring old fortress."

Jackson leapt up and hugged his dear brother. "Thank you! Thank you! I've learned my lesson. Let's get my gold and use it for great things."

Silas smiled wide. "I was hoping you'd change your mind. Let's get to work!"

THE END

FUN QUESTION

If you discovered gold, what would be the first thing you bought with it? Why?

OPTIONAL LESSON READING:

Did you know, Jesus told a story of a person like Jackson who stores up treasure for himself only for it to be taken away quickly? Jesus warns us that riches only provide happiness for a little while– and they can be taken away any day. Instead, He tells us to use what riches we have to love God and love others. The reward for being generous in this way can't be taken away.

SERIOUS DISCUSSION

If you were the richest person in the world, how would you use your riches to help people?

Tomorrow's story has a girl wear muddy shoes to school and church.

CLEAN AS MUD

JESUS RESTORES
1 JOHN 1:9

In tonight's story, Aliyah learns that cleaning can be difficult without the right kind of cleaner.

Not long ago, Aliyah was watching her favorite video stream.

"Welcome to the J-Dan livestream!" said the man on screen. "Whoa! There's over a million of you watching this video right now! But only three of you will be lucky enough to get my newest shoe design – the J-Dan 3000s." J-Dan held up a pair of shoes in the video for everyone to see.

Aliyah gasped at the dirty, muck-covered shoes.

"That's right!" J-Dan said with a laugh. "They are dirty. Everyone *else* has clean shoes. Don't you want to be different? Don't you want to have fun in the mud and not have to clean up afterward?"

Aliyah nodded in agreement. He was right. She wanted the shoes for herself! But J-Dan made his own shoes using a 3D-Printer. There would only be three pairs ever made.

"I'll choose three people who comment on this video to receive a pair," J-Dan said. "And I'll even send along my patented Mud Spray to keep your J-Dan 3000s looking dirty."

Aliyah wrote her comment and was surprised to receive a reply the very next second.

"You're a WINNER! You'll receive the J-Dan 3000's by drone tomorrow," J-Dan messaged her. "Don't wash them. If you do, you must return them. Be proud to be muddy!"

"I will!" she replied before screaming in excitement.

The next day, the drone arrived with a bright white shoe box and Mud Spray tied on with a black ribbon. The shoes themselves were just as dirty as they had looked on the video, but the mud was now dried and crusty. She tried them on, but didn't like the crunch, crunch, crunch every time she stepped.

Determined to do what J-Dan had asked, she took out her Mud Spray, aimed it at the left shoe, and SPLUUUURG!

Fresh mud splattered the entire shoe in speckles and gobs, black, brown, and creamy green. SPLURG, SPLUUUURG!

Now they looked truly horrible. When she put them on, mud squished between her toes.

Aliyah gazed at the muddy shoes in the mirror. To her, they just looked gross. Maybe without the mud, they'd be stylish.

She really didn't like them, but she thought her friends might, especially when they found out they were J-Dans. And if her friends thought she was cool, it would be worth it to wear the muddy things.

But when she wore them to school, kids told her she looked cool, only to then laugh behind her back. "I can't believe she wore them to school…" they whispered.

Her friends felt bad for her. "They look like they might be pretty cool – if they weren't so muddy. Why don't you clean them?"

"I'm not supposed to clean them. If I do – I have to return them. I have to keep spraying them or they get caked to my ankle."

She sprayed the shoes again – SPLURG – just as Mrs. Victor showed up with a frown. "I followed the muddy footprints here, and it looks like I found out who made the mess. Now hand over that Mud Spray and clean those shoes!"

"Yes, Mrs. Victor." When Mrs. Victor walked away, Aliyah turned to her friends. "Now I'm stuck. I'm supposed to *clean them* and *not* clean them."

Her friends did some hard thinking. "Maybe you don't have to clean them at all. Maybe you can just cover the dirt with something else."

Brilliant! Paint!

Aliyah found white paint in the art room and painted over the mud. But the mud blended with the white, making a swirled, brown goopy mess that was even worse.

She asked her friends what to do.

"Maybe you can make them dirtier, but with something less dirty than mud."

With a fresh idea in mind, Aliyah ran to the cafeteria and looked through the fridge. *Hmm...milk!* GLUG-GLUG! Some of the mud washed off, but it made the shoes soppy and gross – and they smelled like cow!

"Now what can I do?"

Her friends did more hard thinking. "Maybe if you do everything with them that you do with clean shoes, they'll eventually be clean without you having to clean them."

She had to try. And she knew just where to go.

She went to church.

She always wore nice, clean clothes to church.

So she wore them up and down the aisles, ignoring the shoeprints, acting happy. She didn't make a face when she smelled the milk or when the mud squished through her toes.

But that didn't help either.

She started to cry.

The pastor came to her and asked her what was wrong. He listened to her explain everything. "You know, I used to leave a stinky dirty messy trail behind me everywhere I went," he said when she finished.

"Really?"

"Yeah. Not with shoes. For me it was my sin. I did so many bad things, it was like spraying mud on muddy shoes, over and over. Then, I'd try to make myself look better by going to church or saying nice things to others, but really, I was messy inside. It's kind of like how you tried to clean your mud with paint and milk. Doing good stuff doesn't take the bad away."

"What did you do?"

"I asked for Jesus' forgiveness. Nothing else will do. When He forgives me, it's like He washes away all the sin I've put on myself. He washes my sins away still today."

"Thank you! I understand. But my shoes..."

"Do you want them to be clean?"

Aliyah contemplated before answering. "I do."

"Then we'll use water. Just like Jesus' forgiveness, you need lots of it, and you just have to ask."

"But I'll have to return them."

"You might. But let's get you clean first. Then maybe we'll convince J-Dan to try a design that doesn't mess up school carpets."

THE END

FUN QUESTION

What would be the most fun thing to do in the mud?

OPTIONAL LESSON READING:

Did you know, Jesus is the greatest cleaner of all time? The Bible says in 1 John that Jesus can cleanse us from sins. Sins make us dirty, just like the Mud Spray made the shoes gross. We might try to cover up our sins or pretend we're clean – like Aliyah's friends told her to do with her shoes – but we can't clean ourselves from sin on our own. But if we go to Jesus in prayer and ask for His forgiveness, He'll wipe our sins away!

SERIOUS DISCUSSION

Have you ever had to clean a really hard-to-clean mess or stain? Are our sins hard to clean, too? How so? (We can try lots of things, but only one thing works).

Tomorrow's story sees Michael go on a chase to save his missing fox!

THE MINUS ONE

GOD PURSUES US

LUKE 15:3-7

In tonight's story, Michael shows us how each one of us is extremely important to God.

Not long ago, one of Michael's 100 foxes ran away. This was odd for two reasons. First, it was odd that Michael had 100 foxes to begin with, but he loved foxes more than anything. He treasured them and treated them like family, giving them love and care above and beyond what they needed. That's the second reason it was odd that a fox decided to run away.

"I have to find Cinder!" Michael moaned, searching high and low.

"Well," said Michael's friend, Sergei. "At least you have 99 other foxes."

Michael frowned, beginning to count the foxes a fourth time. "But I'm missing one! Wouldn't you be upset if you were missing just one finger even if you still had nine others?"

Sergei looked at his hands before shrugging. "But this is different. These foxes are all here and want to be here." Then he pointed to where paw prints led to a hole dug under the foxes' wall. "The one that left thought you and this place weren't good enough for him. Maybe he deserves to be out there."

Michael gasped as he ran to the wall, looking into the Great Forest where hungry eagles hunted foxes. Not seeing Cinder, he turned back to Sergei. "So what if he does deserve to be out there? I love him." Michael's lip trembled. "It's not safe for him out there. I've got to go after him."

With that, Michael grabbed his emergency backpack and darted away, following the paw prints into the forest. Sergei called after him, but Michael was focused on one thing only – finding Cinder.

He barreled through the forest at top speed, crashing through low-hanging branches and leaping over fallen logs. The paw prints zig-zagged all the way to the river, where Michael threw out his grapple drone, hanging onto it as it carried him over the water.

"Cinder!" he called out, searching the water that rushed below his dangling legs. He searched and searched until he saw an orange streak that had to be fox fur.

Suddenly, a shadow passed over him and a large bird shrieked from above. "CAWW!"

Michael yanked the grapple-drone's handle and swerved just as a giant eagle swooped down with sharp talons extended.

The bird flapped its massive wings, turning in mid-air for another attack. It didn't like the drone. It wanted Cinder for itself!

Thinking fast, Michael searched for a landing area. There wasn't anywhere to land except for…a kayak! Michael dropped from the drone as the bird clutched it with its talons.

He plopped into the kayak, next to the surprised kayaker. "Hey."

"Hey," said the kayaker. "Is that your fox?"

Michael spotted the fox on the other end of the kayak. "Yes!"

But as soon as Cinder the fox caught Michael's attention, he yelped, leaping into the water and swimming to the shore.

Michael's heart dropped. Cinder didn't want to be caught. It was true. But still, Michael had to catch him before the eagle did. "After that fox!" Michael commanded.

And the chase continued. When Cinder ran from the shore, up the mountain, Michael followed. When Cinder fled down the snowy mountain in a skier's backpack, Michael followed on a snowboard.

When Cinder scurried into the ski resort, out the front door, and onto the city bus, Michael was right behind – only a few seconds too late. He had to rent a bicycle and pedal like mad to catch up.

By then, he was exhausted and battered from the journey. Still, he didn't give up. The determined eagle was hovering above, waiting for the right moment to strike.

Michael pedaled next to a motorcycle and grabbed on. He pointed at the bus. "My fox is on there!"

And the chase continued to the airport, where Cinder bounded onto a plane with big letters on the side reading "SKYDIVING LESSONS."

"Cinder, wait!" Michael yelled as the fox's tail disappeared inside. But it was too late. The plane took off, leaving Michael behind.

Still, Michael didn't give up. He gave every last dollar he had to another pilot and was soon up in the air in a plane next to Cinder's. He opened the side door and yelled across the open air to the sky divers preparing to jump from Cinder's plane.

"CINDER!"

Cinder poked his head between one of the skydiver's legs and yelped at seeing Michael. Maybe he had been too frightened, or maybe he liked the chase – either way – Cinder leapt right off the plane.

"No!" Michael screamed. He snatched a parachute and leapt out after the falling fox.

The two fell and fell, hurtling through the clouds toward the ground below. Michael could look down on Cinder below, who now seemed frightened, whimpering and yelping, thinking he was alone and helpless.

The fox's frantic escape may have been exciting at first, but it wasn't any longer. It now could see how badly it could end.

And it only got worse.

CAWW! The eagle had been waiting.

It streaked through the clouds, ready to pluck its meal from the sky.

But Michael was there, rocketing forward, snatching Cinder into his arms before the eagle could snag him.

Soon, Michael was hugging Cinder close as they gently floated toward the ground under their parachute. Seeing that Cinder was now in Michael's protection, the eagle retreated.

Cinder was shaking, but he was no longer trying to run.

When Michael got home and told the story, Sergei was awestruck. "Whoa. You care that much about one little fox? You would pursue him through forests, over lakes and mountains, on kayaks, buses and airplanes?"

Michael smiled. "Sure. God loves and cares about me so much, he pursues me even when I sin against Him. So I know how much one little fox can appreciate that kind of love."

THE END

FUN QUESTION

If you could design a racecourse around your town (city) where would it go? Would racers ride anything during the race?

OPTIONAL LESSON READING:

Did you know that Jesus told a story like this one but with a shepherd who pursues a lost sheep? The shepherd loves each one of his sheep just like Michael loves each one of his foxes. This is just like God's love for you. Even though there are many more than 99 kids in this world, He loves and pursues (chases after) YOU, even if you "run away."

SERIOUS DISCUSSION

Why do you think Cinder the fox kept running from Michael? Though you might not run away from God with your legs, are there times you'd rather do things your way instead of God's? Pray now; tell Him you want to stay close to Him.

Tomorrow's story has a science experiment in a dark, dark room.

THE TRUTH IN THE ROOM

THERE IS ONE TRUTH

JOHN 18:38

In tonight's story, Charlotte learns that believing something or feeling something doesn't make it true.

ot long ago, Charlotte was astonished at her mother. "You signed us up for *what?*"

"An experiment. But it's not the kind of experiment with chemicals or anything dangerous. The scientists will give you, Tamara, and Camila a problem and watch how you solve it."

Her mother's words calmed Charlotte. What she said next made her excited. "And by helping the scientists, they will give you $100."

Charlotte jumped up and down, clapping. "Will Tamara and Camila get $100, also?"

"They sure will! In fact, would you like to go shopping before the experiment?"

"For sure!"

Charlotte, Camila, and Tamara, with their three mothers in tow, began their shopping trip downtown, not far from the New York City Laboratory. They were given one hour to shop in whichever store they chose, and their first choice was The Elegant Dress Shop.

Charlotte didn't really like dresses much, but she was happy to help her friends find the dress of their dreams. Camila tried on pink ones, red ones, ruffled ones, frilly ones, and a silly rainbow one.

Tamara ruffled through racks and racks of dresses, searching for the right one. "Nope. Nope. Def nope! Not happenin'! Nope! No…wait. YES! I found it!"

Charlotte came running. "Let me see."

Tamara held up a majestic white and silver dress that seemed as if it were taken from a Disney movie. It sparkled as it turned, glimmering bright in Tamara's eyes.

"Tamara – you're so beautiful," Charlotte gushed when Tamara tried it on.

Tamara twirled, ogling at herself in giant mirrors. "I'm not Tamara anymore. I'm Princess Tamara of New York."

Charlotte scrunched her face. "Huh?"

"That's who I am. I was born to be a Princess. This dress only proves it."

Charlotte exchanged looks with Camila, who shrugged.

"You *look* like a princess," Charlotte said calmly.

"No, I *AM* a Princess," Tamara replied sternly.

Charlotte didn't back down. "I'm sorry, but shouting something doesn't make it true."

"I believe it's true! I feel it! How could you say that I'm not when I feel it so much?"

Charlotte sighed. "Believing something doesn't make it true. Neither does feeling it. It's just not true."

Tamara was disgusted and ready to blow just when the mothers arrived, shepherding them to the experiment. Charlotte didn't have time to settle things with Tamara before they were standing in a bare, white room with a scientist in a white lab coat standing before them.

"I'm going to bring each one of you to a different part of the room, and then the lights will go out. Stay right where you are and wait for instructions."

Charlotte did what she was told. Tamara was across the room, and Camila to the side. Suddenly, the room went completely black. It was so dark that she couldn't even see her fingers when she held them to her eyes.

The scientist's voice came through a loudspeaker as a whirring sound rumbled near her feet. "There is one object in the middle of the room. I will instruct you to reach up, one at a time, and feel what is in front of you. Then tell me what the object is. Charlotte – go first."

Charlotte was nervous. She had no idea what she might touch. But she reached up, into the dark, and found a thin, leathery object. It was long, and rope-like. Though it would be the oddest rope she had ever felt, she had no other guess.

"It's a rope," she said.

Then, to Charlotte's surprise, her friends gave different answers. Very different answers.

"It's a spear!" Camila said.

"It's a fire hose!" Tamara said. "I don't know what you two are thinking! It's clearly a fire hose. Too soft to be a spear. Too thick to be a rope. I'm right. You're both wrong!"

Charlotte was confused and wanted to argue back but figured there was something they were missing. And she was right.

"Believe it or not," began the scientist, "you are all touching the same thing."

"Not," Tamara moaned.

"Right now, you all believe you know the truth. You feel you are right. But there is only one absolute truth that you are blind to see. Do you want to see?"

Charlotte nodded, but then remembered that the scientist probably couldn't see her nodding. "Yes!" she shouted.

The lights came on so fast it forced Charlotte to cover her eyes. Then, slowly, she opened them to see something almost magical.

It was an elephant.

A real, live elephant, hidden behind glass except for the windows where the three girls could reach to touch it. And now, Charlotte could see how they had arrived at three very different answers.

Charlotte had been feeling the elephant's rope-like tail.

Camila had been feeling one of its spear-like tusks.

And Tamara had been feeling its hose-like trunk.

"See," said the scientist with a smile. "Thank you for your assistance."

The girls went back to their mothers where they excitedly shared the experiment from beginning to end. Charlotte was happy that it was over and extra happy to have the $100 in her hand.

Tamara snapped her $100 dollar bill as she skipped toward The Elegant Dress Store. "I'm gonna get my princess dress."

"Oh, right," Camila said. "I forgot. Should we be calling you Princess Tamara of New York?"

Tamara shrugged. "Nah. That whole elephant thing got me thinking. I really *want* to be a princess. And I thought I could believe it hard enough to make it happen. But really, when the lights are on, I'm not daughter to a king – so I'm not a princess."

Charlotte gave her friend a hug. "But it can still be fun to pretend." They shared smiles before dashing into the store.

THE END

FUN QUESTION

What have been your favorite things to pretend to be?

OPTIONAL LESSON READING:

Did you know Jesus said the reason He was born and came into the world was to tell us the truth (Jn 18:38)? The truth must be VERY important, right? It is. Many things in the world can fool us, like the dark room fooled Charlotte. But like the scientist turning on the light, Jesus lights the way to show us the truth. If we follow Him and His teachings, we'll never be fooled!

SERIOUS DISCUSSION

If Jesus came to show us the truth, what do you think Satan is trying to do (trick us/lie to us/deceive us)? Jesus calls him the Father of Lies for a reason! Let's make sure we are on the side of truth, never telling lies!

Tomorrow's story has a bank robber who uses a jet pack to escape!

THE ROBBER AMONG US

WE ARE NOT OUR WORST MISTAKE

MARK 2:16–17

In tonight's story, Stetson learns that God loves every person, even if they've done rotten things.

Not **long ago,** Stetson was riding his bike to youth group with his friend Grady. They were passing the bank when the alarms went off.

WAH! WAH! WAH!

The alarm was coming from inside the bank. The boys skidded to a stop and stared. Nothing appeared odd at the bank. The doors were closed. There wasn't any smoke. What was…?

BOOM! The doors burst open, and a masked man came flying out, wearing a jet-pack and carrying bags that were overflowing with money.

Stetson and Grady ducked as he flew overhead and blasted into the sky. A security guard came running out of the bank, chasing him, but the rocket robber was already gone.

"Whoa! We have to tell the youth group what we just saw!" Grady exclaimed.

They raced to the church and put on their name tags before running inside their youth room and telling everything they'd seen to their friends and Pastor Walt.

"We should pray for him," Pastor Walt said to the boys' surprise.

Grady scoffed. "For the Rocket Robber? You mean, we should pray that he gets caught, right?"

Walt nodded. "Yes, that he gets caught, but also that he can stop sinning and find what he needs in Jesus instead of through stealing."

Over the next week, Stetson heard more stories of the Rocket Robber. Each new robbery, Stetson got an update on his phone with the news. *Beep!* He'd robbed a bank in Celina. *Beep!* He'd robbed a bank in Montezuma. *Beep! Beep! Beep!* He'd robbed three banks in three other nearby cities and got away every time.

It was at youth group during game time that the news of the Rocket Robber's capture showed on his phone. *Beep!* Stetson alerted the whole group. "He got caught!"

The kids quickly gathered around, watching the video that showed the moment a police drone fired the net that wrapped around the Rocket Robber, taking him to the ground. It showed the police surrounding him, putting him in handcuffs, taking off his mask.

"That's Max's dad!" Grady exclaimed to everyone's shock.

Gasps rippled through the crowd as they gazed at Max.

Max seemed horrified, more surprised than anyone. "No. No, it can't be."

"That's definitely your dad," Grady said. "How could you not know he's a criminal? Your family suddenly get rich? Your dad start smelling like jet fuel?"

"He's a good man!" Max said before bursting into tears and running away.

Pastor Walt followed after Max.

Stetson felt sorry for his friend. Especially since Stetson's own father had once committed a crime.

It had been a long time ago, before Stetson was born, but his dad had gone to jail for a big mistake. He'd faced the consequences, repented of his sins, and done everything he could to not make the same mistake again. And Stetson loved his dad more than anything. He was the best father he could imagine.

While Grady was laughing and whispering to the others, Stetson interrupted. "*Everyone* messes up."

Grady snorted. "Yeah? Not like, 'Oops, I robbed five banks.'"

The other kids laughed but stopped when they saw Pastor Walt returning.

"I've done worse than that," Walt said with a sad look on his face.

Grady cocked his head. "Huh?"

"It's true. I've lied. I've sinned. I've broken the Creator of the Universe's commands many more than five times. And for every one of his commands I break, I deserve horrible consequences, even worse than the Robber might get."

He took out name tags and slapped them on his own chest. They read LIAR. SINNER. LAW-BREAKER. "I could put these name tags – these labels – on me. Is that who I am?"

The kids shook their heads.

"They don't tell the whole story, do they? I'm not just my worst mistakes. It's the same with the Rocket Robber. He's not just a criminal. He's also a human. God's creature. Someone's son. And he's a father."

Stetson nodded, hoping other people knew his father was more than just a criminal, too.

"It's the same for all us," Pastor Walt continued, "because we have all broken God's commands at one time or another."

Pastor Walt walked around and put labels on every one of them.

THUMP! Stetson felt the SINNER label thump his chest. It didn't feel good seeing that. Other people looked at his label as well. *THUMP!* LAWBREAKER went on Grady's chest. He grimaced.

"It doesn't feel good to have everyone see just your most rotten part. You are so much more!" Pastor Walt wrote on more tags and put them next to his old ones. HUMAN. BELOVED. GOD'S CHILD. REDEEMED. FATHER.

"Don't look at me and just see my worst label. Don't look at the Rocket Robber and just think he's a criminal. See him as God sees him. In God's eyes, we are all His children who are horribly lost without Him. Jesus came to help those who most need Him. And right now, Max's dad needs Him."

Stetson sighed, feeling like he should say something. "My dad was a criminal, too."

Grady shot him a look as the others gasped.

"He didn't rob banks, but he went to jail," Stetson explained. "He made a huge mistake, but he's asked for forgiveness and done good things since then. He's still my dad, and I will always love him."

"Really?" Grady asked, quietly. "I didn't know. He's such a cool guy."

Stetson shrugged. "He still is." Then he pointed to the label on Grady's chest. LAW-BREAKER. "We're all messed up and make mistakes."

"I get it," Grady said. "Sorry I laughed at Max and his dad."

Pastor Walt smiled. "Apologize to Max when you get a chance. But for now, let's pray for their family."

THE END

FUN QUESTION

What sport would be the most fun if players could also wear jetpacks? Why?

OPTIONAL LESSON READING:

Did you know that Jesus hung out with people who were known to be awful sinners? They might as well have had big labels on them saying BIG BAD SINNER, STAY AWAY! But that wouldn't keep Jesus away. He came to seek and save sinners. He isn't afraid to love people like the Rocket Robber. He loves them and wants them to sin no more!

SERIOUS DISCUSSION

How would you feel if you had to wear a giant label on your chest that said HORRIBLE SINNER for ten days? What would your friends say? If your friend wore the label to school or church – would you still hang out with him/her?

Tomorrow's story has two kids fall through a tunnel into a hidden room.

THE MASTER'S PIECES

ALL PEOPLE ARE BEAUTIFUL

PSALM 139:13-14

In tonight's story, Penelope sees why God loves every one of His special creations.

Not long ago, Penelope's class boarded a school bus for a field trip. Mrs. Yarmush wouldn't tell the class where they were going. Instead, she typed in the destination on the autobus controls and took her seat.

It wasn't until the autobus pulled up to the Art Museum that Penelope's friend, Silas, let out a groan. "No wonder she wouldn't tell us where we were going. No one would have gotten on the bus," he complained. "Except for you."

He was right. Penelope shrieked for joy. She loved art – the old stuff from history long ago and the new.

Penelope smiled and leapt for joy as they climbed the steps.

Even an hour into the tour, Penelope was excited for more. Their tour guide, Mr. Gilroy, had led them through three exhibits already, but he now led them to the main attraction – a giant hall filled with sculptures on both sides. Colorful paintings decked the walls, and digital pictures scrolled underneath their feet.

"Now we enter the Gary Oliver Drumwell Wing. Drumwell is the world's most famous artist. His works are everywhere and are widely regarded as the most beautiful. You are very lucky children to see it."

Penelope gaped at the beauty all around her, even as Silas snuck a peek at his cell phone. Other kids sighed and tried to stomp the animals in the pictures at their feet. Mrs. Yarmush scolded them and stopped the class for another lecture, giving Penelope a chance to walk onward, closer to the sculptures.

Silas snuck alongside her.

The first sculpture was a beautiful woman in a red dress. Pony-tail, long nose, thick eyebrows. Pregnant. A young child clung to her side.

The sculpture looked like stone, but also shone, like it was lit inside. It appeared real, as if the woman were flesh and blood. Every wrinkle had been captured, in her skin and in her dress. Locks of hair gleamed and fell at her ears.

"Wow!" Penelope awed.

But Silas was already moseying to the next one. Then the next. Each one was very different. Finally, he settled on a statue of a girl and made a face at it.

He leaned to whisper to Penelope. "Why'd he make ugly statues?"

Then, all of a sudden, a voice boomed through loudspeakers. "HOW DARE YOU!"

Silas jerked and swiveled left and right, searching for a place to run – and a person to run from.

But there was nowhere to run.

The last thing Penelope saw before vanishing into a dark hole was Mrs. Yarmush reaching out for her – and Mr. Gilroy waving goodbye.

She fell and fell and fell through the trap door until she felt herself begin to slide, down and around, twisting and twisting until light revealed a giant room with vats of bubbling liquids, crates of woods and stones and metals, and walls of every tool she could imagine.

Silas bumped into her as they both stopped at the end of the slide, marveling at the gigantic workshop. And there, working on a statue with a chisel and hammer, magnifying goggles, and a messy apron, was Gary Oliver Drumwell. Penelope would recognize him anywhere.

"You called one of my masterpieces…UGLY?" he said, glaring at Silas with eyes that seemed to bulge inside his goggles.

Silas stammered. "Well, I, uh, I-I-I was just saying…"

"It was insulting. If you put down one of my beloved creations, it is putting *me* down. Do you know how much time and effort I put into each one of my works? Do you know how much I love each and every one?"

Silas glanced around and shrugged. "A lot?"

Gary laughed. "It sounds like you need a real tour."

"Oh, please!" Penelope begged giddily.

Mr. Drumwell led them to an area brimming with rolls of paper, sketches, and a giant mirror. "This is where I imagine each and every creation. The animals, plants, landscapes, and humans that I create start as an idea. Then I craft them, pondering every detail. Each and every one is unique – and special to me."

The artist grabbed a stack of papers and showed them to Silas. On them were sketch after sketch of the girl Silas had called ugly. "I designed her just how I wanted her. I had many other options, but I chose to make her THAT way. It is what I wanted – what I thought was beautiful. And you called it ugly."

Silas hung his head.

Mr. Drumwell continued, taking them by the chemical vats and crates of stone, wood, and metal. "I then start creating the piece. And every part of it is important. The inside, even though you don't see it, holds it all together. And sometimes…"

He held a flashlight up to a dreary, gray statue. When the light hit it, it shone a brilliant, golden orange – like a sunrise was inside of it. "…sometimes the inside shines through."

Penelope was in awe as Mr. Drumwell continued the tour, showing them how he crafted each statue, each painting, each creation with care and precision and love.

"Finally, I put my signature on each one." Mr. Drumwell handed Silas a pair of glasses and pointed at the statue's shoes. Silas hunched over and peered at the shoes until he gasped.

"It's your initials!"

The artist smiled. "That's right. Now, if you look hard enough at your classmates, even without glasses, you'll see that each one of them is one of God's masterpieces. He created each one of them with great care – and He loves them all dearly. I don't think He'd like to hear you call one of *them* ugly, would you?"

Silas gulped. "No, sir."

"Good. Now you two had better run back to your class." He said, pointing at a dark staircase. "I've got to get back to work."

THE END

FUN QUESTION

If there were a museum with all of the creations you've ever made, what would be the best creations in it?

OPTIONAL LESSON READING:

Did you know the Bible says God knit you together in your mother's womb? That means that God created you bit by bit. You are wonderfully made – a wonder! If someone says something upsetting about your body, it bothers God as well. You, and everyone you see, are special masterpieces that you should treat with honor and respect, because we all are God's precious artwork!

SERIOUS DISCUSSION

What are some things you say to an artist about a beautiful work of art (great painting, beautiful drawing, amazing Lego creation)? Have you ever praised God for how He made *you*? Try it now. You're a masterpiece!

Tomorrow's story has two boys who must escape a crumbling path by making a hard choice.

THE TWO PATHS

FOLLOW GOD'S WORD

PROVERBS 14:12

---

*In tonight's story, Kelvin learns that God's Word is a better guide
than our own eyes.*

Not long ago, Kelvin trudged along the rocky path in the dark, exhausted and scared like the lines of others beside him.

He glanced back in the faint moonlight, only to see more of their path crumble and fall into the nothingness below. He had to keep marching forward with the others, or he would fall into nothingness, like Manny had just hours ago.

Like the rest of them, Kelvin had been marching for days. None of them knew what was going on or how they had gotten there, but they all knew they had to keep going. Kelvin didn't know most of the others, but he'd stuck close to his best friend, Trey, since the beginning.

"Why are we here if the nothingness is just going to catch us?" Trey complained. "I don't know how much longer I can just keep walking and walking."

As he often did, Kelvin looked at the dirty, worn instruction booklet he kept close at all times. He could barely see the words with only moonlight to light the thin pages. "The book says we're here for a good reason."

Trey grunted. "That book looks like it's been lying around for hundreds of years. What does it know?"

"It's gotten a lot of things right so far. It even said Manny would fall."

Trey shrugged, looking forward again as whispers of surprise bubbled from the crowd ahead. Kelvin instantly saw why.

There was light.

Real, glowing, beautiful golden light up ahead.

Not only that – the path split into two. One wide path curved away and led leisurely downhill toward the light. There were guardrails on its sides to protect those who walked its smooth ground. There were also fruit trees and fountains springing along its sides. It appeared to be a glorious, welcoming path.

The other path led away from the light, uphill at hard angles. It was jagged and rocky, and even darker than before. Yet it continued on as far as the eye could see.

The crowd reacted with joy, rushing toward the wide path. Many plucked fruit from the branches and drank from the fountains. Trey began to pull at Kelvin, urging him toward the wide path.

"There's food and drink and light," Trey said, "but we must hurry. We don't have much time to enjoy it."

But Kelvin's mind was buried in the book. "This says that we need to choose the narrow path. The wide path leads to destruction, but the narrow path leads to life."

Trey peered at the book, reading the same words. Then he gazed at the two paths. "But look. Which path looks like it leads to destruction? Are you going to believe some old book, or your eyes?"

Kelvin examined each path and saw what Trey was saying. Kelvin, too, longed for the fruit and cold drink. He wanted to walk downhill. He wanted something easier than what the narrow path offered. Who would tell him to go somewhere more difficult? More painful?

Who? Kelvin wondered. *Who* wrote this book?

He turned the book to its cover and found the author. Astonished by the name, he gaped at Trey. "My dad wrote this book."

Trey thought about that for a long while, but when another loud crack carried away more of the Earth, Trey shook away his thoughts and started toward the wide path. "I don't know your dad – but I do know what I see."

"No!" Kelvin called. "Don't! That path leads toward destruction!" Surer of himself than ever, Kelvin begged and pleaded with anyone who would listen.

But none did. All were moving forward, downward, enjoying the food, drink, and ease of their new lives, even as the Earth crumbled behind them.

Kelvin called for them until his voice was hoarse and until the chasm of nothingness got too close for comfort. Then he started his long, arduous trek up the narrow path. It was slippery and full of sharp rocks. He cut his legs often but had to keep trudging upward and onward.

There was little time for rest. His throat hurt from lack of water. His eyes hurt from straining for light. Yet he continued, climbing farther from the wide path, determined to reach the top for his father. It was what he wanted. And he always knew what was best.

From high above, Kelvin could see the wide path below more clearly now, how it wound slowly toward the bright light. He could even see Trey, though he looked as small as a bug from so far away.

Kelvin smiled, thinking of his friend, but only for a moment – for his eyes wandered toward the light. And blinking slowly, he realized what the light was.

It was fire.

It was a bright, hot furnace.

And it was the end of the wide path. There was no other way for Trey to go. Nothingness to the left and right, and nothingness coming at them fast from behind.

CRACK! The way back to the narrow path crumbled away leaving no way back for Trey.

"Trey!" Kelvin screamed.

But he was too far away. From where Trey was, he couldn't see that the light was a fire. Trey had no way of knowing he was doomed. The only way he could have known was…the book. It had told them the way, but Trey hadn't believed.

Kelvin couldn't watch his friend go toward the fire.

Instead, he trekked onward and onward until finally, after what seemed like forever, he reached the top.

Suddenly, someone removed his virtual reality goggles, and Kelvin realized he was in the astronaut training room. Trey was there, too, shaking his head as he realized how he'd messed up.

Their instructor held out the instruction book astronauts had to follow to survive on other planets.

"So, I hope you learned your lesson. Follow the instruction book."

THE END

FUN QUESTION

What is your favorite book? If you could be one of the characters in it, who would you be?

OPTIONAL LESSON READING:

Did you know that the Bible warns us about a path that leads to death? It also says that that way *appears* to be right just like the wide path looked right to Trey. The path the Bible warns us about isn't a real path you can walk on, but a lesson we can learn. Trust God and His word even if there *appears* to be a better way. His way will always be better in the end.

SERIOUS DISCUSSION

Have you ever played with a one or two-year-old? What kind of things do they do that they THINK will be great – but could actually harm them (eating small toys, going toward street)? All humans are like this, and God is like our wise parent. Let's listen to Him!

Tomorrow's story has an invention that gives three girls special new abilities.

Talent Patches

Using Our Gifts For Him

Matthew 25:14-29

In tonight's story, Riley learns that talents are a gift that we can use to help others.

Not long ago, sisters Riley, Nora, and Chloe were working quietly on their homework when they heard an explosion below their feet. The floor shook. The pictures on the wall rattled. And smoke poured from the basement door.

The three sisters immediately knew something had gone wrong with one of their father's experiments. He was a brilliant inventor, but his ideas often failed many times before working. But never before had there been such a loud explosion and so much smoke.

"Dad!" Riley called as he burst through the door, collapsing to his knees.

The girls rushed to his aid, coughing as the smoke billowed into the living room. "Dad, are you all right?"

Their dad coughed and removed his goggles. His face was covered in black soot. He appeared tired as he held out a shaking hand.

"Here," he said with a shaky voice. There were three circular patches in his palm. "Take one. Put it behind your ear. They are my gifts to you."

The bewildered girls each took a patch as their dad coughed again. "I only managed to save the three. The rest – everything else is lost. I trust them to you."

Riley carefully put her patch in her pocket and stayed with her dad until the ambulance arrived. She stuck by him all the way to the hospital where he would need to stay until he recovered. The doctors said it would be a very long time.

After a few days, the girls had to return to their home, saddened by the absence of their father and confused by what he had left them. Riley took her patch from her pocket. Nora and Chloe did the same.

"I suppose we should do what he wanted. Put them behind our ears," Riley said.

The girls agreed and slowly stuck the patch against their skin.

Colors danced across Riley's eyes, like a hundred rainbow sprinklers had set loose in their house. "Wow!" she exclaimed.

Nora began to sing beautifully, more beautifully than any singer she'd ever heard. And Chloe grabbed a marker and began writing long strings of numbers on their markerboard. "I can see how math works. It's everywhere. It's beautiful!" Chloe said.

Riley saw beauty in colors instead and started to draw. She found paint and began to design and shape the images that came to her energized mind.

It was hours later that the girls stopped and awed at what they had done. Riley had created beautiful paintings. Chloe had used numbers to solve problems. And Nora had recorded beautiful new songs.

"Whoa. These patches. They've given us new talents," Chloe said. "Very different ones. But amazing ones."

"We have to take good care of them," Nora said. "Because these are the only three like this. And our father gave them to us."

"When he recovers, he'll want the patches back," Riley explained.

Nora shrugged. "But we don't know when that'll be. We should probably put them to good use until then."

And that's what the girls did – some more than others.

Nora used her voice talent to join the youth group worship band. She sung beautifully in front of others, helping others worship God. When someone recorded her performance to the internet, millions of people were able to hear her words praising God and teaching truth about who He is.

Chloe used her talent with numbers to build computer apps. One app helped ambulance drones get to sick people faster. Others helped people find clean water. Another helped predict tornadoes so people could seek shelter before they hit. She made loads of money from all these apps, but she gave it away generously to those who needed it.

Riley, though, had a different idea of how to use her talent. She drew and painted amazingly beautiful creations of all kinds, but she was careful not to lose her artwork. Her room became the most amazing art gallery in the world. If her art had made it outside her door, people would have marveled at the beauty of God's creation in new, fresh ways.

But Riley was afraid. She was afraid that someone would see her talent and find out about the patch. And if they found out about the patch – they would steal it. And then, when her father recovered, what would she say to him?

So she kept her creations, her talent, to herself.

Until, finally, the day came when her father came home.

"Girls!" he shouted cheerfully, embracing them. "I'm finally back, and I'm so glad to see you. I love you more than anything."

After many hugs, their father noticed Nora's patch. "Ah, yes! You still have your patch! How have you used your talent?"

Nora told him of all her performances, of all the people who heard more of God's truth and grace because of her singing. And his face glowed with joy. "Well done, daughter."

Chloe was next, telling him of all her math work and how it had helped sick people, thirsty people, and people in need of shelter. He smiled wide when she told of how much good her talent had produced.

"Well done, daughter," their father said again.

Riley's heart was beating fast. She was nervous. "Father, I kept your patch safe. I made beautiful creations for you, and I have kept them safe as well!"

Her father smiled, but she noticed it wasn't as wide as when he had heard the other girls' reports. "I love you, Riley, no matter what! And I'm glad you kept it safe. But talents are meant to be shared. I made these patches to produce talents that would spread love, peace, joy, truth, and kindness to others, just as Nora and Chloe did."

Riley began to cry, but her father embraced her. "Don't worry, daughter. You still have the patch, don't you?"

She nodded vigorously.

"Then let's see how you can use it for good."

THE END

FUN QUESTION

If you could choose one of the three talent patches, which would you choose? (Art, Music, Math)

OPTIONAL LESSON READING:

Did you know that Jesus has given you talents? It's true. He has given them to you – and one day He'll ask you how you used them. Many people use those talents to get themselves money or other rewards. Others just hide their talents, afraid that they'll fail. But you will be different. You will use your talent to share love, truth, and joy with the world, won't you?

SERIOUS DISCUSSION

Name some people and their talents at your church (or school). How are they using their talents to help other people?

Tomorrow's story has a video game amusement park with a very rewarding contest.

SHOW ME THE LOVE

HELPING OTHERS

MATTHEW 25:31–46

In tonight's story, Kordell learns that knowing someone will help you love them better.

Not long ago, Kordell lazily sat on the couch, holding his game controller, playing the video game WorldMaker with his friends online. They were building a block fort together, complete with lava dumps, crossbow traps, and diamond rocket tubes.

Kordell had fun talking with his friends through the headset, but it wasn't the same as playing with them outside. On sweltering hot 100-degree summer days, though, staying inside was the best option.

Suddenly, LeMarcus' shrill voice rang in Kordell's headset. "Hey, guys. In the sky!"

Kordell made his blocky video game character look up until fireworks came into view. They were bursting in all colors, making fun shapes. Then a special WorldMaker character they all recognized appeared riding a dragon.

"It's Benefact! The greatest WorldMaker of all time!"

He appeared with his usual suit and tie. "Hello, people of Littletown! Tomorrow, my real-life amusement park opens – WorldMaker Land! And because you are faithful players, you are invited to the opening!"

Kordell had to turn down the volume as his friends, LaMarcus and Murphy screamed for joy into their headsets.

"That's right. Only one thousand kids get free tickets. You'll find them in your inbox. And don't miss this – there's a contest where the winners will get free tickets FOR LIFE. Want to hear how you win?"

Kordell leaned in, holding his breath in tense excitement.

"While at the park on opening day," Benefact began, "whoever *shows they love me the most* will be the winners. That's it! See you there!"

The boys discussed the contest for hours and prepared into the next day. When they approached the majestic theme park, they were dressed in WorldMaker shirts, with Benefact's style of suit and tie painted on, along with headbands and sunglasses with Benefact's name on them. They even painted their faces with Benefact's character. Finally, they carried flags with his name on it, waving them as they ran toward the entrance.

"We love you, BENEFACT!" they shouted as they were given wristbands, granting them entrance to the park.

They were so excited about the park and so loudly shouting Benefact's name that they didn't notice the man in tattered clothing, holding a cardboard sign asking for help.

In fact, they were excited all day, and just as absorbed in showing their love for Benefact. They came up with songs, praising Benefact's name while they waited in line. "Bene-bene-BENE-FACT, how mighty is your name! Bene-bene-BENE-FACT, our love for you's insane!"

But while they were singing, they didn't notice the lost boy looking for his parents.

Murphy held a banner with Benefact's name the entire roller-coaster ride – every loop, upside-down three times. He never let go, and he never stopped screaming "We love you!"

But he didn't notice the girl who dropped her money while going upside down on the roller coaster. She didn't have enough money for lunch, while the boys bought an extra funnel cake to place at the feet of Benefact's character statue.

By the end of the day, the boys were confident they had shown their love for Benefact more than anyone. By all appearances, they loved Benefact very much. Their voices spoke of their love at loud volumes. And they'd even given him a funnel cake.

So, when the loudspeaker called the thousand boys and girls to the front entrance to hear the contest announcement, they were confident.

"Fellow WorldMakers!" boomed Benefact's voice. "Thank you for coming to my park. Many of you really love me. But sadly, many of you don't really know me as well as you think you do."

Kordell frowned and eyed his friends with concern.

"That's right," Benefact continued. "If you really knew me, you would know *how to love me*. You show your love for me by loving those who are in need."

Kordell sighed in despair. He had forgotten all about Benefact. He was the most giving, loving person in the world.

"So, I watched today to see who would show their love for me by loving those who were weak, scared, lost. Like the man without a home at the park's entrance. Like the boy who had lost his parents. Or the girl who lost her money and couldn't buy food. Those who loved those little ones truly love me."

Benefact showed videos of other kids helping those people in need. Kordell was sad that he had neglected them.

"But," LeMarcus began loudly, drawing Benefact's attention, "We sang songs to you, waved your banner high, and gave you funnel cake!"

Benefact smiled. "Thank you. But if you do those things without love for those I love, they aren't what I desire. Now, please check your wristbands. Those that turn green may enter in my park, for free, for LIFE. Those that turn red, you must go home."

The three boys watched their wristbands turn RED.

Their parents gave them comforting hugs before taking them back home, far from the joyful sounds of World Maker Park.

THE END

OPTIONAL LESSON READING:

Did you know that Jesus will one day ask us how well we showed our love to Him? There are many ways to love Jesus, but if you know Jesus well, you'll know that He loves to serve people in need. So a really good way to show Jesus you love Him, is to find people who need something, and love them like He does! This means, every time we serve someone, we are loving Jesus!

SERIOUS DISCUSSION

If Jesus asked you how well you were serving people, how would you answer? Do you think you've missed any chances to love people in need at school/church/sports?

Tomorrow's story has a boy who goes on a crazy spending spree with his father's money.

THE COMEBACK KID

GOD'S UNCONDITIONAL LOVE

LUKE 15:11–32

In tonight's story, Cai learns that loving someone when they don't deserve it is called grace.

Not long ago, Cai and his brother Cooper were reaching under their parents' bed for their fumbled football when Cai noticed a strange box. He reached for it.

"Hey!" their Dad scolded. "We told you guys to stay out of our room." His eyes were upset at first but melted into amusement when he noticed the box in Cai's hand.

"What's this?" Cai asked, giving the heavy box a shake.

Their dad took the box and stared at it like it was something dangerous. "This box has your inheritance in it."

"What's inheritance?" Cai asked.

"It's the things or money given to children after their parents die."

Cai stared at the box with new importance. "So, whatever's in that box will be ours when you die?"

His dad nodded seriously.

"Can we see what's inside?" Cai asked.

Cooper gasped. "No! Don't open it! I don't want Dad to die!"

Their dad hugged Cooper. "It's okay. I'm fine and won't be dying any time soon. If you want to see inside, you can." He then placed his palm on top of the box. There was a loud beep, and something unlocked. Fascinated, the boys leaned over their dad's shoulder to see the contents.

Inside were two silver cards. That was it. Nothing else.

"That's it?" Cai asked in astonishment.

"Yup. That's it. Two cards for my two boys. They are like computer piggy banks full of digital money, and each has control over half of all the money I have."

His father's words hung in Cai's mind. *Full of digital money.* That meant that card could buy him things – lots of things – SO many things! But would he have to wait until his father died?

"Can I have it now?" Cai asked excitedly.

Their dad looked hurt. Cooper was shocked and confused. But Cai's mind was so swirling with the possibilities of what he could do with the money that he hardly noticed.

After a long pause, his father stared hard at Cai. "I've worked a long time for this money and kept it safe for you. It is wise that I keep it safe for you until you are older, wiser, and more ready for it."

Cai sulked. He didn't want to wait. He wanted the money almost more than he wanted his father.

"But…" his father began, brightening Cai's mood. "…if you want it now, you may have it. It is meant to be yours after all."

"YES!" Cai shouted without another thought, and he quickly grabbed one of the cards.

He hugged his father and brother goodbye, packed a bag, and was off on the grandest spending spree of all time.

Cai started by buying a wing suiting tour over the pyramids. Then he para-skied in the Alps. He jetpacked around Yosemite National Park and rode a drone-donkey through the Grand Canyon.

But after flying all over the world, he decided to settle down in the World Largest Mall. Using the card, he paid for all of his friends to stay in the hotel attached to the mall where they slept. Most of their time was spent shopping, playing at the arcades, riding the amusement park rides, battling at laser tag, riding go karts, and eating at the amazing restaurants.

Cai had the greatest month of his life. Thirty days of happiness.

And then his card ran out money.

"I'm sorry," said the hotel manager, handing back his card. "Since you can't pay for any rooms, you and your friends need to leave immediately."

Just like that, it was over.

Cai's friends wished him luck and left. His belly rumbled, but he didn't have enough money for food. He had his suitcase, but nothing else. At night, he slept under a bridge to keep out of the rain. His clothes became dirty and tattered.

Soon, he found himself back in the mall scrounging for scraps in the garbage cans. Any food sounded good to him, even soggy burger buns.

A janitor caught him scrounging and offered him a job cleaning the bathrooms. He gladly took it, scrubbing toilets so that he could get enough money to buy food.

One night, while scrubbing a nasty toilet, he began to weep. He missed his friends and the fun they had, but more so, he missed his father and his brother.

But would they ever take him back? Cai had taken the money card from his father and left, like he didn't even care about his family. All he had cared about was himself.

Cai had taken everything his father could give, and he'd given nothing in return. And he still couldn't give his father anything. Even if Cai came back to his father, he'd have an empty card and filthy clothes.

That's it.

But he had to. He loved his father. Cai *had* to ask for his forgiveness, even if there was a small chance he'd say yes.

So Cai used what little money he had left to buy a ride part of the way home. Then he walked the rest. He walked until his shoes were falling apart. His hair was matted with dirt. He stunk. And he knew his heart stunk, too.

But when his father saw him approach from the porch, he didn't seem to care about any of that. His father ran to him, swept him into his arms, and kissed his dirty, stinky face. "My son! My son! You've come back!"

And they wept together.

"I will prepare your favorite foods and invite all our friends. We will have a grand party – after you take a long bath!"

Cai couldn't believe it. "I…I don't deserve any of that. I took all that you gave me and turned my back on you."

His father wrapped him in another hug. "It's called grace, son. And if you come to me, I'll always welcome you as my own."

THE END

FUN QUESTION

If you could have a giant sleepover with all of your friends anywhere in the world, where would it be? Why?

OPTIONAL LESSON READING:

Did you know that Jesus told a story like this one, but the son ends up in a pig sty before coming back to his father? That son, like Cai, had to realize how much he stunk before deciding to head home. We all are like that. We need to realize how much our hearts stink – how badly we need Jesus – so that we can go to him even after we've messed up. And He'll be waiting!

SERIOUS DISCUSSION

Have you ever hidden from a parent or caregiver after you've done something wrong? Why? What should you do instead? (Go to parents/God, ask forgiveness).

That's the last story for this volume. Thanks for listening!

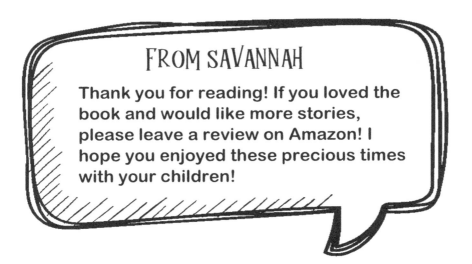

FROM SAVANNAH

Thank you for reading! If you loved the book and would like more stories, please leave a review on Amazon! I hope you enjoyed these precious times with your children!

Here's the link to review:

https://bit.ly/5MinChristian

Thank you!

Savannah Bloom

Made in the USA
Las Vegas, NV
02 January 2024

83807986R00059